I'm
Not
Invited?

To anyone, or the friend of anyone,
who's ever felt left out

Atheneum Books for Young Readers
An imprint of Simon & Schuster Children's Publishing Division
1230 Avenue of the Americas
New York, New York 10020

Book design by Sonia Chaghatzbanian
The text of this book is set in Mrs. Eaves.
The illustrations are rendered in watercolor.

Manufactured in China
First Edition

10 9 8 7 6 5 4 3 2 1

Library of Congress Cataloging-in-Publication Data
Bluthenthal, Diana Cain.
I'm not invited? / Diana Cain Bluthenthal.
p.   cm.
"A Richard Jackson book."
Summary: Minnie is upset when she is not invited to Charles's party.
ISBN 0-689-84141-8
[1. Parties—Fiction.] I. Title.
PZ7.B62726 Im 2003
[e]—dc21   2001031650

I'm Not Invited?

Story and pictures by Diana Cain Bluthenthal

A Richard Jackson Book
Atheneum Books for Young Readers
New York London Toronto Sydney Singapore

"What time is the party?" Kathleen said to Charles as they whizzed home on bicycles after school Tuesday.

"One o'clock, Saturday," Charles replied.

Minnie's ears perked up. "Charles is having a party!" she thought.

She ran all the way home from the bus stop to see if her invitation
was waiting.

But there was nothing in the mailbox for her except an overdue
notice from the library.

"Hmm," Minnie said, staring into the long, metal tunnel.

In the kitchen, the phone was ringing.

"Charles!" she squealed when she heard his voice.

"I'm so excited. I heard that you're . . ."

"Growing worms in science class!" Charles finished. "Are you too?" he asked.

"WORMS?!" Minnie shrieked.

"Mealworms, actually," Charles said in a rush. "But I lost my list of things to bring to school tomorrow. Do you have one?"

"A worm?" said Minnie.

"No!" said Charles. "A list of things for worms: a jar, a lid with holes, some crushed cereal. . . . Never mind. I'll call you back and explain later."

"It's not his birthday on Saturday," Minnie kept thinking as she started on homework. She knew his was in June, like hers.

Minnie looked at the new vocabulary words for Friday's spelling quiz.

dig
rig

dump
truck
concrete
load
build

PARTY!

balloons
cake
candles
decorations
favors
games
goodies

guests
invite
presents
prizes
streamers
surprise
wish
wrap

23

"I hope Charles calls me back soon," she said.

That night during supper, the phone rang.

"I'll get it!" said Minnie, jumping from her chair.

"Who was it, Min?" asked Minnie's mother when Minnie returned.

"It was Parties 'R' Us," said Minnie.
"They had the wrong number."

As she dressed for bed, Minnie noticed that the pattern on her pajamas looked a lot like confetti and streamers.

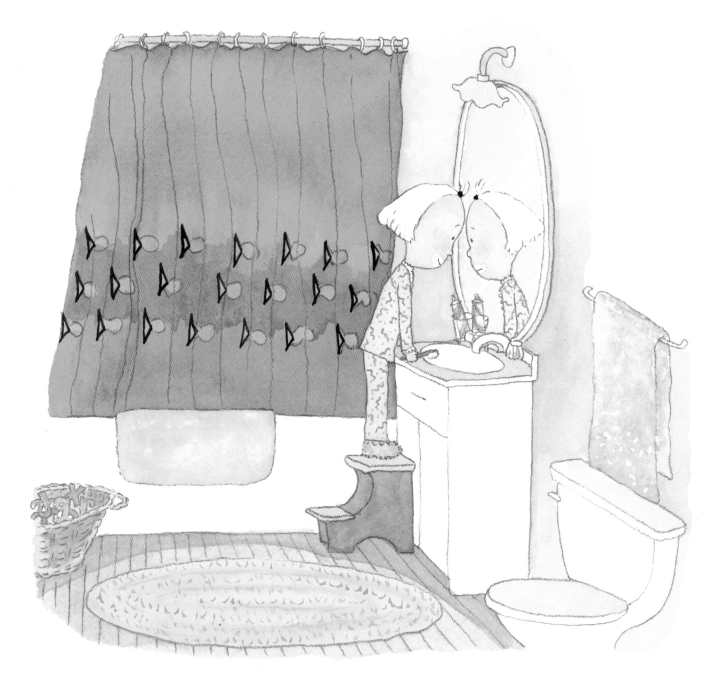

"We'll see Charles tomorrow," she said to the mirror, "and I'm sure he'll invite us then."

On Wednesday, Minnie didn't see Charles at school all day.
That afternoon, she raced home to check the mailbox.

That evening, she tried concentrating on vocabulary words.
But she couldn't.

Minnie worried about her missing invitation.
"Did it go to the wrong house?" she wondered.

"Or something worse?"

"Think *positive*," she told herself.
"It will come tomorrow."

On Thursday, Minnie did receive a note from Charles.
It said:

Dear Minnie,
I named my mealworm after you!
I thought you'd like that.

Your friend,
Charles

But it didn't say anything
about a party.

She set the table for supper, counting the days until Saturday:
one, two, and a half . . . one, two, and a half.

Minnie's father looked around, puzzled.

"Something's missing," he said.

"Garlic bread?" asked Minnie mother.

"No," said Minnie's father. "Minnie's smile."

Minnie lifted the corners of her mouth a little,
but she made a frown on her plate with her spaghetti.

After supper, Minnie practiced for the next day's quiz.

In bed she wrote out the words once more. "Maybe the party was canceled," she thought. "Or maybe Charles's mother said he could invite six guests, and I was number seven."

"It's okay," she said. "I don't have to be invited to everything."

By Friday morning, Minnie felt miserable.

She forced herself to eat breakfast, knowing her mother would protest if she didn't.

Especially on a quiz day.

But as she sat watching her cereal turn soggy in the milk, something occurred to her. Something wonderful.

"Maybe he thinks I'm already invited," she thought.

"That's it!" Minnie shouted. "Charles meant to invite me, but forgot to, and then forgot that he forgot!"

Minnie slumped down again.

"And that's terrible," she moaned, "because how do you ask someone if he meant to invite you?"

Minnie's class took their spelling quiz right before lunch.

Minnie was glad to get it over with.

She was in the cafeteria eating her sandwich when she saw Charles standing in the hot-lunch line.

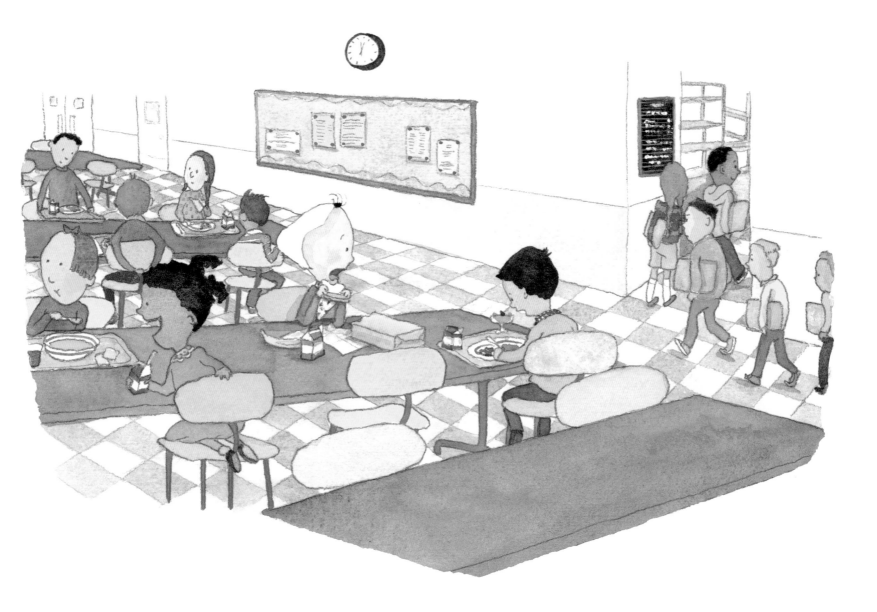

Gathering courage, she went after him. She was just about to speak
when she felt a tap on her shoulder.

"NO CUTTING!"
said two mean-looking boys.
"GO TO THE BACK OF THE LINE!"

At the end of the day, the teacher
returned the quizzes.

Minnie's paper read "A+! *Nice work!*" but a tear fell down her cheek anyway. It dropped off her chin and landed on the word *invite*.

That gave Minnie an idea.

When the final bell rang, she hurried like crazy to the buses.

"Charles!" she yelled when she saw him coming. "Look!! Look!!
An *A+* on my spelling quiz! Come and see! Come and see!"
Minnie hoped with all her heart that when Charles read the words
he would remember. . . .

"SIT DOWN!" growled an angry voice behind her.
It was the mean-looking boys from the cafeteria.
"AND STOP BRAGGING!!"

"Charles!" Minnie cried as the buses started to rumble.
"Have a nice weekend! Especially Saturday!"

Then all Minnie's hopes
sank straight to her stomach.
It was no use.
"No invitation, no party,
no nothing," she wept.

Minnie ate very little supper, and went to bed early.

"Cat's got your smile again tonight, Min?"
said Minnie's mother, coming to tuck her in. "An A+
on your spelling quiz. . . . Now there's something to be sad about."

"It's not that," Minnie whimpered, rolling the quiz
into the shape of a party hat.

"Hmm," said her mother. "Then something else must have
happened at school today."

"It's what didn't happen," said Minnie.

Minnie's mother leaned in close. "I know how you feel," she said. "I don't like it when things don't happen either. That's why I'm thankful for tomorrows."

She kissed Minnie on the nose.

"But tomorrow is Saturday," Minnie replied.

Saturday morning, Minnie rode her bike to Charles's house.
Her heart pounded the whole way.

When she arrived, she saw balloons and more balloons.
"Oh, no!" Minnie cried, "I'm not invited!"
She pedaled sadly home.

In the kitchen, the phone was ringing.

Minnie hoped it might be Charles, wanting to know why she wasn't at the party.

"Hello?" she answered.

"Hi, Minnie," said a voice, but it wasn't Charles's.

"Some of us are playing kickball at the dirt field later, if you want to come," Kathleen told her.

"Thanks," Minnie said.

"At least I'm not the only one missing the party," she thought.

"I think some dirt could do you good," Minnie's mother agreed.
"And will you please try to lose that long face while you're out there?"
"I'll try," said Minnie.

At the dirt field, all the kids divided up into teams.

Minnie kept thinking of Charles, wondering what games they were playing at his house.

Just then, there was a rustling in the bushes.

"CHARLES!" Minnie gasped.
"What are you doing here?! Why
aren't you at your party?"

"It's not my party," said Charles,
"and our house is a ZOO. I had to ESCAPE!"

"Oh, Charles," Minnie cried faintly. "All week long
I thought that you were . . ."

"Going to be at my sister's party?" said Charles. "No WAY.
I'd rather be here any day!"

Minnie smiled big.

"Me too!"

she said.